Imagine Harry

Written by

Kate Klise

Illustrated by

M. Sarah Klise

Harcourt, Inc. Orlando Austin New York San Diego Toronto London

Library of Congress Cataloging-in-Publication Data
Klise, Kate.
Imagine Harry/written by Kate Klise; illustrated by M. Sarah Klise.
p. cm.
Summary: After Little Rabbit starts school, he sees less and less of his
invisible friend, Harry, and finally tells his mother that Harry moved away.
[1. Imaginary playmates—Fiction. 2. Rabbits—Fiction.] I. Klise, M. Sarah, ill.
II. Title.
PZ7.K684Ima 2007
[E]—dc22 2005035079
ISBN 978-0-15-205704-6

First edition
A C E G H F D B

Printed in Singapore

The illustrations in this book were done in acrylic on Bristol board.
The display type was created by M. Sarah Klise.
The text type was set in Brioso.
Color separations by Colourscan Co. Pte. Ltd., Singapore
Printed and bound by Tien Wah Press, Singapore
This book was printed on totally chlorine-free
Stora Enso Matte paper.
Production supervision by Jane Van Gelder
Designed by April Ward

For best friends,
real and imaginary,
everywhere

Little Rabbit had some very nice friends.
But he had only one *best* friend: Harry.

Some of the other animals called
Little Rabbit's best friend *Imagine* Harry.
But Little Rabbit just called him Harry.

In the winter, Little Rabbit
and Harry played in the snow.

In the spring, they rolled down the
gentle hills of soft grass that surrounded
Little Rabbit's house.

In the summer, they swam ...

…and climbed trees.

When it was hot, Little Rabbit asked Mother Rabbit for two glasses of lemonade—one for him and one for Harry. When it was time for a snack, Little Rabbit asked for four cookies.

"Well? Harry gets hungry, too," Little Rabbit explained to Mother Rabbit, who almost squashed Harry by sitting on him. (That happened a lot.)

Little Rabbit never sat on Harry.

On nights when Harry wanted to stay up past his bedtime, Little Rabbit said that *he* had to stay up past his bedtime, too. "Someone has to keep Harry company," he told his mother.

When Harry didn't want to have his hair washed,
Little Rabbit said he didn't want *his* hair washed, either.
"We might get soap in Harry's eyes," Little Rabbit warned.

Once, when Mother Rabbit fixed brussels sprouts for dinner, Little Rabbit said he couldn't have any on his plate. Harry didn't like the smell.

"Your friend Harry is starting to wear out his welcome," Mother Rabbit said.

"*Shhhhh!*" Little Rabbit whispered. "You're hurting Harry's feelings. Besides, Harry always has very nice things to say about *you*."

In the fall, Little Rabbit started school. He asked Mother Rabbit if Harry could go, too. "Harry can go to school, but he won't get his own desk," Mother Rabbit explained. "He'll have to sit with you and be very quiet." "He'll be good," Little Rabbit promised.

And Harry was. In fact, Harry was so quiet
on the first day of school that nobody noticed
him sitting at Little Rabbit's desk.

And when a classmate passed out birthday
treats, Harry told Little Rabbit that he didn't
need a snack.

(Harry was thoughtful that way.)

Most days, when it was time to eat lunch in the
cafeteria, Harry stayed behind in the classroom so
Little Rabbit could sit with his new friends.

And then one day, during a particularly fun
music class, Harry whispered softly in Little
Rabbit's ear, "I'm tired. I think I'll go take a nap."
"Okay, Harry," Little Rabbit whispered back.
"See you later."

Shortly after the first snowfall, Little Rabbit was invited to an ice-skating party.

When he returned home, Little Rabbit told
his mother all about it.

"It sounds like a wonderful party," Mother
Rabbit said. "Did Harry have a good time, too?"

Little Rabbit was startled to realize that he
hadn't seen Harry in weeks.

"Harry moved away," Little Rabbit said. "He's got his own house now."

"Oh," said Mother Rabbit. "He's certainly welcome to visit anytime."

But Harry never came back to visit the Rabbits.
Sometimes at dinner, Little Rabbit and Mother
Rabbit talked about him.

"Harry doesn't have a phone at his new house,"
Little Rabbit said. "And he never learned how to
read or write. So I guess we won't be hearing from

Little Rabbit made many new friends that first year of school. He didn't think about Harry very much— except once in a while in the spring, when the smell of new grass reminded Little Rabbit of the hills he and Harry used to roll down together.

Harry loved doing that.